HAUNTED ISLAND PART 1

WHAT'S THE MYSTERY ??

MMUDLIYAR UDAY KUMAR

Made with ♥ on the Notion Press Platform
www.notionpress.com

Haunted Island

[In Treasure Hunting office]

*Ram is the chairman of treasure hunting office .
He called Rohit to his office .*

Rohit : Can I come in sir ??

Ram : Yes , come in ...

Ram : Rohit take your seat .

Rohit : Yes sir ..

Ram : I have a plan Rohit .

Rohit : What is the plan sir ??

Ram : You have to take your team to Porion Island .

Rohit : What ???

Ram : Yes . That Island was closed so many years that is why no people and tourister not went there . So there can be any precious treasure .

Rohit : Sir think before taking decision ..

Ram : Why ??

Rohit : Because it is Haunted

Ram : I know it ...

Rohit : Sir why to take risk . We will search treasure in India why to go Italy ??

Ram : Rohit . What is our team motto ??

Rohit : Not afraid of anything ..

Ram : Then

Rohit : Sir there are many men's in our team . If anything happens to them then who will be responsible for their family??

Ram : Nothing will happen ..

Rohit : But sir ..

Ram : It's my order ...

Rohit : Ok sir ..

Ram : Wait !!!!

Rohit : Yes sir ..

Ram : I will give advance cash as a 1 crores to you and you will distribute to your team 10 lakh as advance and remaining I will transfer after the mission is successfully completed .

[Rohit went to his team]

Rohit : Guy's I have a deal .

Team : What's the deal ??

[Than Rohit told all thing's about it]

Team : We think it is risk so we need 12 lakhs as advance ....

Rohit : No ...

Team : Rohit than forget us ...

Rohit : Okay . Last 10 lakhs please ...

[After thinking long time]

Team : Okay . Rohit because you are our friend that's why we accepted the deal ..

Rohit : Ok guys . Tomorrow we will go from here by ship .

Team : Ok .

[At night they packed all thing's including gun's , knives , ammos and sword .]

[At ship]

Pratap : Tomorrow by 10.00 PM night we will reach the Island .

Team Of Rohit and Rohit : Ok .

[Day 2]

[Finally the day came that they reached to the Island]

Rohit : Team today night we will stay in ship from

tomorrow we will put the tent .

Team : Ok ..

[At Island]

One man was running from there . By shouting " Help me"

[Next Day]

[At morning]

Rohit : Good morning guy's .

Team : Good Morning Rohit .

Rohit : First of all let's search a place which is plain . Where we able to put the camp . Beside camp our Tent's .

Rahul the team member of Rohit : Bro , see at the top a big bungalow is there . Let's go there .

Rohit : Really ??

Rahul : Yes bro see from here .

[After that Rohit saw the bungalow which was top the hill .]

Rohit : Ok guy's let's go up ..

Team of Rohit : Ok .

[While climbing up to top he was thinking that " In this Island ghost and zombies has been being that information got from google search. But]

[After that they reached to top of the hill]

Rohit : Guy's let construct the camp here .

Team : Ok ..

[After that they saw that the bungalow was locked from out]

Rahul : Bro the bungalow is locked from out .

Rohit : Try to break the lock .

Rahul : Ok .

[After few minutes]

[Rahul was not able to break the lock]

Rahul : It is not breaking bro ..

Rohit : Oh shit !! ....

Rohit : Take this gun and shoot the lock .

Rahul : Why bro . We don't know whose bungalow is this then why to break this lock .

Rohit : I can understand . But when this island is closed from many years who will be living inside ??

Rahul : But !!

Rohit : I am your boss and it's my order ...

Rahul : Ok ..

[After that he took the gun from Rohit and broke that lock . Suddenly the bat's came out ..]

Ramesh : Rohit . Bat's are coming out . I am running from here something bad thing is going to happen .

Rohit : Then give your advance 10 lakh and run away .

Ramesh : No .

Rohit : Then keep quite .

Rohit to his men's : Guy's let's go inside .

Team : Ok ..

[After that they went inside]

They were searching for a place where they can keep their remaining weapon's . After that they found a place .

Rahul : Rohit see here we can keep our weapon's .

Rohit : Yes it is safe place .

[It was Kitchen . In kitchen in a particular cupboard .]

[After that they started fixing the light's ...]

[After that they fired bonfire outside the bungalow . Because it was night and it was winter season . The temperature was around 19 degrees .]

[Rahul brought the barbeques with him .]

Rahul : See I brought a small tandoor means barbeque .

Ramesh : Ohh !!! Today means our party ??

Rahul : Yes .

Rohit : What you will do with barbeque ?? When you not brought anything for cooking ??

Suresh : Yes .

Ganesh : Yes . Rohit is saying right

Jeeva : Yes what you will do ??

Badrinath : I thought today there will be party but !!

Rahul : I have brought the fishes and chicken which is marinated .

All : Yehhh !!!

Rohit : Ok boy's today Rahul is giving party .You all eat your dinner and come to bungalow .

All : Ok

Rahul : You will not eat ??

Rohit : Bring for me inside ..

Rahul : Why ??

Rohit : I will have a small peg .

Rahul : Ohhh!!!

Rohit : I will keep for you .

Rahul : Ok ..

[After that they all started eating it ..]

Rohit went inside the bungalow . He was just seeing from window . Suddenly he saw anything behind grass .

He took his gun . It was tiger which was going at the direction of his friend's . He ran out and shooted the tiger .

His friend's was very afraid .

Rohit : Enough !! Let's go inside and have a sleep .

All friend's took all thing's inside and slept in hall .

Rahul : Here in hall many bed's are there . Is this a bungalow or hospital ??

Rohit : Whatever it may be . Sleep on it . For today . Tomorrow we will throw this out ..

Rahul : Ok ..

[Next day]

Rohit and his team firstly throwed the bed's out

and cleaned the bungalow .

[After 3 hrs]

Rohit : Let's go out with our weapon's . We have to find treasure according to this map .

Team : Map ?? Where you got ??

Rohit : It was inside kitchen in a bad condition .

All : Ok . Now it will be easy to find .

Rohit : No . See here this is teared half .

All : Oh no !!
Rohit : Don't worry . We will find out the treasure and go back to our home .

All : How .

Rohit : Yes . Here some clues are there .

All : For what ??

Rohit : Don't know ...

All : Ok .

Rohit : 1st clue is " In mountain many trees are there few are not there and few are there"

All : Mean's

Rohit : Let's go out and see .

[After that they went to jungle]

Rohit : There are many trees in mountain and some are not there means . I think cutted trees . Let's see ..

After that they found the cutted tress . Which was cutted into half .

[Rohit saw again into map]

Rohit : The clue is " Behind a big stone a tunnel is there "

[After that they went to the place which was given as clue]

Rahul : This is a big tunnel .

[Rohit saw again into his paper]

The clue was telling " Here is the end wait for information "

Rohit : What !!

Rahul : What happened??

Rohit : See this .

[After that they saw that what was written]

Rohit : I think anybody is there inside . Let's go ..

Rahul : No Rohit . If anything strange happens than ??

Rohit : If we get the treasure map than ??

Rahul : There can be chances .

Ramesh : Than let's go inside why to wait ??

Rohit : Ok .

[After that they went inside the tunnel]

They saw that the man was locked into a cage .

Rohit : Hey men !!!????

All Men's started shooting him ..

Rohit : Stop !!!

Rohit : Who are you ??

Men : Take this key and open the lock .

Rohit : Why ??

Man : Please do this otherwise we all will be killed here .

[After that they took the man from there and took him to the bungalow .]

Rohit : Man who are you ??

Man : I am Eddy A treasure hunter . From your team . I am also Indian .

Rohit : Ok Eddy how you was locked there ??

Eddy : It's a big story . I was appointed in India for this work but , But before . Take this map and take the treasure from here .

Rohit : What happened with you ??

Eddy : If I will take it's name . It will come here . So better I will not .

[At night]

[Rohit was confused]

In his mind's " Who is the man and why he gave the map to us ?? this question's were running in Rohit mind .

[He was seeing through his window]

[Suddenly a strange voice came which was very scary .]

Rohit shouted loudly .

All men's came there .

All men's : What happen Rohit ??

Rohit : Nothing ...

All men's : Is all ok ??

Rohit : Ok .

[After that they all went and sleeped back]

Rahul : Rohit are you ok .

Rohit : Yes I am ok .

Rahul : You can't hide it . What happend to you . From your eyes I can see you are afraid of anything .Tell me ..

Rohit : Don't tell to anyone

Rahul : Ok .

Rohit : A strange voice came when I was standing and thinking about Eddy .

Rahul : From where ??

Rohit : From middle of jungle . All animal's was shouting .

Rahul : I think here anything is there . We should run away from here by tomorrow .

Rohit : No ...

Rahul : Why ??

Rohit : If we find this treasure and take it to India than our India will be proud . Because from many years all country people came here to hunt the treasure . But no Information gone back from here . Here if try to go back than also we will not able . Here is no signal . Now all of us has to die here . Now it is depend on us . Because the ship will come after 15 days .

Rahul : I think it will be ghost .

Rohit : No . Impossible . The voice which came was like something else .

Rahul : Let's see tomorrow at afternoon . Now we will sleep . Let's see tomorrow .

Rohit : Ok

[Next day]

Rohit : Eddy where is the map ??

Eddy : See this is the map .

Rohit : It is in next mountain . But there is a rope bridge in middle of jungle which is very old .

Eddy : Yes .

Rohit : Let's go there ..

Men's : Ok ..

Eddy : I will be here you all go to jungle .

Rohit : No . You will come with us . I think you know well about this jungle .

Eddy : Ok .

[The creature which voice was strange what was that ??]

Rohit and his team reached to the bridge . The bridge was full of rope and wood . Somewhere it was broken .

Rohit : Let's go ..

Team : How ??

Rohit : Keep hope .

[After that they passed from the bridge]

[Rohit saw to the map]

Rohit : In this map an underground is there , where the treasure is there . Let's go !!!

Eddy : It's not easy ..

Rohit : Why ??

Eddy : In underground a devil lives who hunt man .

Rohit : What ?? Hunting man ..

Eddy : Yes .

[At late night]

Rahul : See .

Rohit : What ??

Rahul : The hand of red devil . He is coming out .. Let's hide ...

Rohit : Ok .

[After that they hided behind bushes and trees]

[However the red devil saw them]

Red Devil : Now nobody will escape from here .

[After that they started running from there]

The red devil burned the rope bridge . Rohit and his team fall down and floated on water . It attacked Ramesh , Suresh and Kumar . Who were in team of Rohit .

Rohit and his team fell down from bridge of mountain . They reached down to land . When Rohit came in conscious

Rohit : Guy's get up .

[After few minutes they all came in conscious]

Rahul : Rohit now what to do ??

Rohit : First we have to keep ready all thing's for night war . Are you ready ??

His team : Yes !!!!!

[After that in afternoon]

Rohit and his team started searching for food . Rahul went to catch fishes . Ganesh went to search fruit's .

[After few hour's]

Rahul and Ganesh : We brought food .

Badrinath : I also came .

Rohit : Where you went ??

Badrinath : I went to bring wood from trees for the bonfire in night .

[At night]

[Rahul fried fishes without any masala's]

Rohit : After long time we all faced this thing's .

Rahul : How ??

Rohit : When we went to South Camp we forgot our dinner up at mountain .Because our Elephant and other wild animal's attacked our camp . Now again we are here like that .

Rahul : Yes .

All team : Yes .

Rohit : Now what happened to Ramesh , Suresh and Kumar ?? We don't know also ..

Rahul : Captain dinner is ready .

Rohit : Don't call me captain .

Rahul : Why . As a captain I only bargained to you for the work . Not guided properly . Crudely treated to all . Now also I can't do anything as a captain . Now they are in what situation we don't know ?? . When they were attacked by devil there and there only I decided to sacrifice myself . As I will fight for you .

Rahul : Rohit !! take the dinner .

Rohit : Ok !!

Rahul : Rohit what is your next plan ??

Rohit : We have to do all thing's by afternoon . Because the devil will appear in night only .

[Suddenly a saint came]

Saint : No !!

Rohit : Why ??

Saint : Yes .

[But before Ramesh , Suresh and Kumar came with baba / saint .]

[Rohit and his team was shocked]

Saint : I am Italy saint .

Rohit : Yes we of course know it .

Saint : I have a cottage here .

Saint : The red devil can appear at morning and noon also .

Rohit : But we not saw it at morning and afternoon .

Saint : It will kill you all now .

Rohit : Why saint ??

Saint : Because from many years who ever come's here it has killed all . I has god power however stayed here .

Rohit : Saint where you got my friend's .

Saint : When I was practising . I was thirsty . So I went to drink water . Suddenly I found them and brought them to my hut .

Rohit : Thank you Saint .

Saint : Welcome ..

Rohit : Do you know the story of that red devil ??

Saint : Yes .

Rohit : Than tell us .

Saint : Before many year's . Here a hospital was there . At that time in Italy a virus came which was known as plague . Due to which many people were affected and brought to this hospital . Doctor's were not able to do anything about that virus . So that they decided to kill them all .So they were burned alive . At that time Menon a man who known about that treasure . He was forced to tell about that treasure but he not uttered a single word . Doctor's decided to keep him there . Scientist's came to that hospital and test their invention's on him . As one time they made a strong virus which was known as black fever . They put the injection to Menon . At that time they taught that it will not react anything but it was spread all over patient's who were admitted . One of the patient ran away from there . Because of that men the virus spread in Italy again . So doctor's decided to kill the people who were affected to this virus by killing them alive . They burned Menon alive . After becoming a soul . He become the king of all ghost's who were burned by doctor's . Menon forced them to take revenge . So now Menon become a powerful devil . Inside him 1,60,000 men's soul is there .

[Ramesh was crying]

Rohit : Don't cry .

Saint : His life is in the treasure . If we take it from here than we can able to success .

Rohit : How ??

Saint : I will confuse the ghost by bringing it here in my hut . I will a rangoli where the devil will sit and I will start my pooja and kill him . Now it is depend on you .

[Climax]

They reached there .

Rahul , Ramesh , and Kumar went towards it the red devil came out and started going behind them but suddenly Rohit fell down . Because he wanted to save Rahul and Ramesh from devil attack. He was hanging Rahul came and try to save him . But unfortunately Rohit fell down and died . After that remaining team member's brought it to the hut of saint .

Saint started his mantra .

Red Devil : No . Don't kill me .

Saint : No I will .

[After that he keep on going telling the mantra .]

The ghost started disappearing from there .

Devil : I will come back ...

[After few minutes]

The hut was blasted with a loud noise . No one got hurt .

Saint : I have stored this devil in bottle . Let's throw on sea .

After that they took their treasure from there and they saw that there was no boat to go .

Saint : I have a boat take this and go from here .

Rahul : Saint you ??

Saint : I will also come with you .

After that they throwed the bottle in sea .

[After that they reached to a beach]

[From beach they reached to airport . From airport they reached to India with treasure .

[Few days passed]

[At press meet]

Press Reporter Dharma : Excuse me Rahul Sir

Rahul :Yes Mr .

Press Reporter : Sir as we all know that you and your team has done hard work . But you didn't face any paranormal activity ??

Rahul : Of course we have faced . But we can't tell you the thing's which happened there . But the reader's will know .

Press reporter : What ??

Rahul :Yes . You will come to know later .

News reporter : Sir we have heard that you have

faced the devil .

Rahul : Yes . You all will come to know . As I will write a book on it . But never forget to read it . Our one team member has died . He is none another than my best friend Rohit. We have missed him. Our team leader . We even not got his body. He will be still in our hearts . If I have saved him that day than today there will be celebration . But now . Let us forget the celebration . Think about Rohit . From now Rohit is our god . Thanks . But before going a salute to him .

[At Island]

Rohit : Save me !!! I am here .

[The bottle in which the devil was kept it was opened by a fisherman . The devil came out and activated in Rohit Body .

[1 month later]

One tourister came to that Island but he not returned back...

[One more Adventure is waiting]

See in Part 2

The End .....

Story written by : Mudliyar Uday Kumar .....

Author Biography

I myself Mudliyar Uday Kumar . I am the young author . As I have already published 2 books . This is my 3rd book . I am the student of "The Scholar's English High School" . Thanks for reading this book . Don't forget to rate it ..

Soon the part 2 will come ...

Contents

Printed by Libri Plureos GmbH in Hamburg, Germany